# Grandpa Jim's

# Dolly

Written by **James D. Grainger**

Illustrated by **Thomas Giebler**

Jolly
9/18

meg
9/18

*Jim Grainger*

*Grandpa Jim's Dolly*

Written by James D. Grainger

Illustrated by Thomas Giebler

Copyright 2018 by James D. Grainger, dba Grainger Publications

Cover, book, and layout design by Thomas Giebler

ISBN: 978-1-548-92316-7

*This book is dedicated with love to my two granddaughters, Meagan and Emily Grainger.*

*This book is also dedicated to all who have experienced the love and joy of having a soft-coated wheaten terrier in their life.*

*I want to express my appreciation to Thomas Giebler for his excellent illustrations and assistance with many other details. Also special thanks to my wife, Beth, for her help and encouragement.*

**Come along with Dolly and enjoy the many different things she likes to see and do! Help her find her lost bones too!**

**Dolly likes to go for a ride in the car. She sits in the back seat, which is the safest place by far.**

Can you find Dolly in the car?

**Dolly likes to go to town with Grandpa Jim and see the clown. It's amazing what the clown can do with just one balloon or two!**

What did the clown make?

**Dolly** likes to wear glasses. They help her to see the little brown squirrel hiding high up in the tree.

Can you find the little brown squirrel?

**Dolly** **likes to sit with her teddy bear in the great big rocking chair.**

What color is the teddy bear's bow?

**Dolly** likes to sit at Grandpa Jim's feet. She will sit up and beg for a treat.

What color is Dolly's shirt?

**Dolly** likes to sleep on Grandpa Jim's bed with his pillow for her head.

What color is Grandpa Jim's pillow?

**Dolly** likes to sit in Grandpa Jim's easy chair, and often stays and takes her naps there.

What is laying beside her in the chair?

**Dolly** **likes to watch the kites. They are a beautiful sight. Some kites will really catch your eye when they are flying high in the sky.**

Can you find the striped kite?

**Dolly** likes to climb up on Grandpa Jim's lap and give him a kiss or two. By doing this she hopes he will take her to the zoo.

What color is Dolly's collar?

Dolly likes to go to the zoo. The first thing she looks for is the kangaroo.

What does the kangaroo have in her pouch?

**Dolly** **likes the little wagon that Grandpa Jim rents for her at the zoo. She can ride in the wagon and see all the animals too!**

What color is the wagon?

**Dolly** likes to visit the monkeys that live at the zoo.
She knows they like bananas, so she takes them a few.

How many bananas did Dolly take?

**Dolly** **likes to see the giraffes. She thinks they are made all wrong—two legs too short and the neck too long!**

**How many giraffes can you find?**

**Dolly** likes the elephant with four big feet. She brought her some peanuts to eat.

What color is Dolly's bucket?

**Dolly likes to see the lions, but when they begin to roar, she heads for the exit door!**

How many lions are in the cage?

**Dolly** **likes to see the children pet the sheep and give them something to eat.**

How many sheep can you see?

**Dolly** **likes to watch the ducks swim on the pond,
along with the big, white, beautiful swan.**

**How many ducks are on the pond?**

**Dolly** likes to go to the farm and see the horses that stay in the barn.

How many horses do you see?

**Dolly likes to see the roosters. When they begin to crow, she thinks they put on quite a show.**

How many roosters can you find?

**Dolly** loves her two sisters who live a mile away. When they get together, they run and play.

What are the names of Dolly's sisters?

**Dolly** likes to grab Grandpa Jim's sock. She runs and runs and will not stop!

What color is Grandpa Jim's sock?

**Dolly** **loves Shani, her groomer! This is a true statement and not a rumor.**

What color is Dolly's bow?

**Dolly** likes her toys that she can make squeak. It takes a good one to last her a week!

What toy is Dolly playing with?

**Dolly** likes to play with balls. It doesn't matter if they are big or small. She has fun playing with them all.

Can you find the green ball with bones on it?

**Dolly** likes to swim in her pool. It helps to keep her nice and cool.

What color is Dolly's swimming pool?

**Dolly** likes to go for a walk in the park, but she likes to come home before it gets dark.

What color is Dolly's leash?

**Dolly** loves ice cream! At her birthday party when she turned four, she begged for more and more!

Who came to her birthday party?

# HOW TO ORDER

Grainger Publications
P.O. Box 287
Andover, KS 67002

GraingerPublications@gmail.com

# Photo Album

My party!

Loving parents ♡

A kiss for the illustrator!

Snacktime!

My favorite spot!

I love Shani! ♡

Made in the USA
Columbia, SC
01 April 2018